If you're consistently under par on the course, could you also be under par under the covers?

Will a strong sex drive really make your approach to the putting surface easier?

Questions such as these have no doubt plagued the mind of every person who has ever taken club in hand. Some may have even been golfers. It is to those of you whose thoughts have refused to stay on your own backswings, but have lingered to more exotic fairways—and some unfair ones—that THE SENSUOUS GOLFER is dedicated. For in truth the game of golf is an extremely sensuous thing. The constant variety

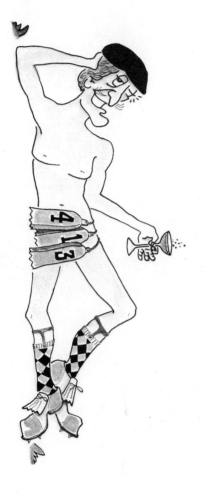

# THE
# SENSUOUS
# GOLFER

by
MARK OMAN

ILLUSTRATIONS BY NIX

Published by Golfaholics Anonymous®
P.O. Box 222357,
Carmel, CA 93922

Library of Congress Catalog Card Number: 76-19347
International Standard Book Number: 0-917346-01-7

Printed in the United States of America

Designed by Kay Cole

FOR BARBARA, who said I
should have my head examined
when I started this book . . .
but thought I should have
something else examined when
I finished it!

# TABLE OF CONTENTS

# word

of terrain, strokes, lies, and penalties a player must negotiate in a round of golf give him the kind of experience that can prove invaluable when participating in one of the more physical contact sports that night.

It should be noted that in many cases the reverse is also true. Simply, your scoring ability the night before may give you a new and unexpected handicap the following day.

Above all, this book is designed to help you grasp the true nature of the sport. When you've mastered the following instruction, you'll be in a position to play a round with the best of them . . . if not on the course, then at least on the couch!

MINERAL SPRINGS

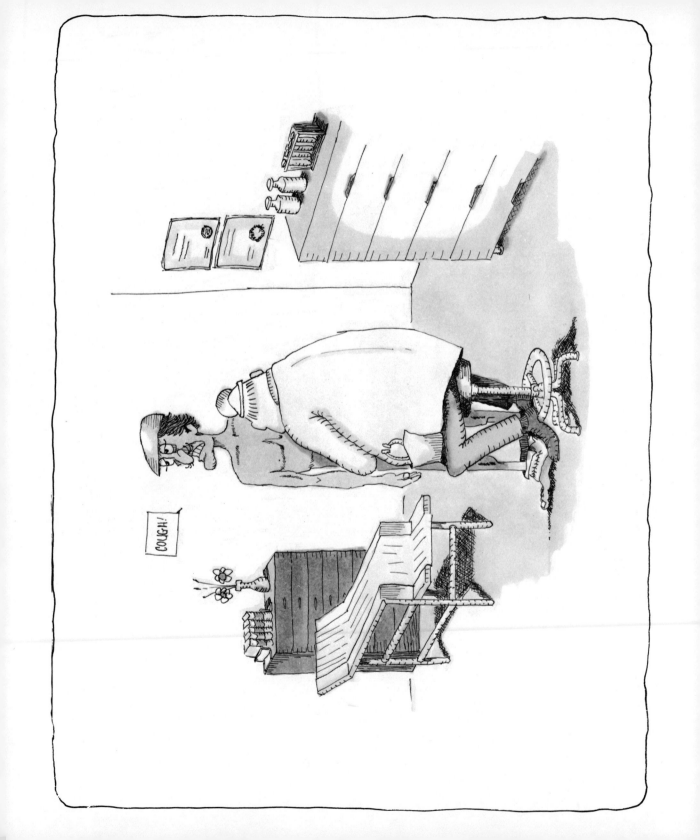

# PART ONE

## YOUR EQUIPMENT

Your golf clubs are like the various parts of your body. Some you have more confidence in than others. Fortunately, you have a choice when it comes to selecting your golf equipment, so there is really no excuse for clubs and balls that don't get the job done to your satisfaction.

# HOW YOUR CLUBS CAN HELP YOU

A player must be properly equipped. It is a sad fact that the players who need all the help they can get in scoring are often hopelessly handicapped by their clubs.

One should realize that even though most sets are matched, different sets have different characteristics as to weight distribution, length and flex of shaft, and the shape and lie of the clubhead.

How weight is distributed between the head and shaft determines swingweight, which should give you some idea of how heavy things will get when you swing it.

Shafts come in different flexes, from very stiff to whippy. What flex will suit you will depend primarily on factors of age, strength and how fast you swing . . . not to mention how often! It has generally been observed, through trial and error, that the slow, deliberate swinger needs a whippy shaft; the fast swinger a stiffer one. Experiment to find which is best for you.

"SHAFTS COME IN DIFFERENT FLEXES . . ."

## CARE OF YOUR EQUIPMENT

There is no question that for maximum control, always keep your clubface clean and grooves free from dirt. Wash with soap and water, but remember that use of a harsh brush, abrasive, or steel wool may damage the chrome . . . among other things.

You should also be careful that your equipment is kept where it won't get banged up and abused. There's nothing worse than going out to play and discovering your shaft is bent out of shape.

4

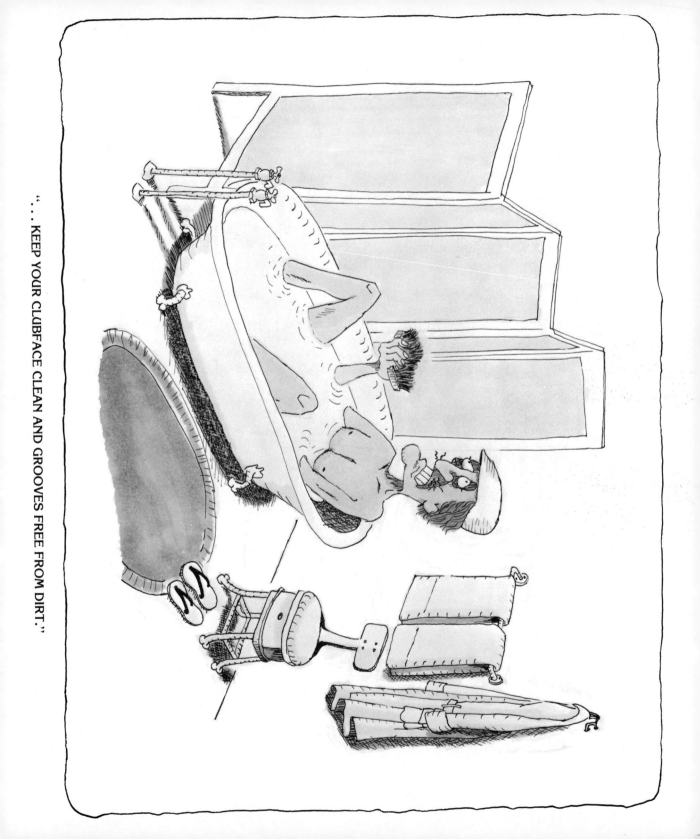

"... KEEP YOUR CLUBFACE CLEAN AND GROOVES FREE FROM DIRT."

# THE GOLF BAG

Many swingers form an attachment to their very first bag and keep it around for years in spite of the fact that their equipment doesn't fit in it the way it used to.

Almost invariably, the older a player gets, the heavier his bag gets. It is at this time that a few of these senior sports decide to put aside their faithful old bag and try one of the newer, more lightweight models, usually with an abundance of synthetic material in their construction.

Some players keep several bags handy, calling upon one or the other depending on conditions of play anticipated. This is usually the sign of a low handicap or very smooth swinger.

"...ONE OF THE NEWER, MORE LIGHTWEIGHT MODELS..."

# HAVE A BALL

Other factors being equal, the distance your ball will carry is determined by how much it is compressed. The question everyone asks is, "What can ball compression do for me?" Well, that depends on the type of swinger you are.

Hard swingers need a hard ball. Softer balls have a somewhat different feel at impact. They tend to stay on the clubface longer and are easier to control making them a much better ball for beginners and easy swingers.

But compression and distance shouldn't be your only consideration. Durability is also important over the long haul.

The important thing is to select your balls carefully, for once you begin to play, you're stuck with what you've got!

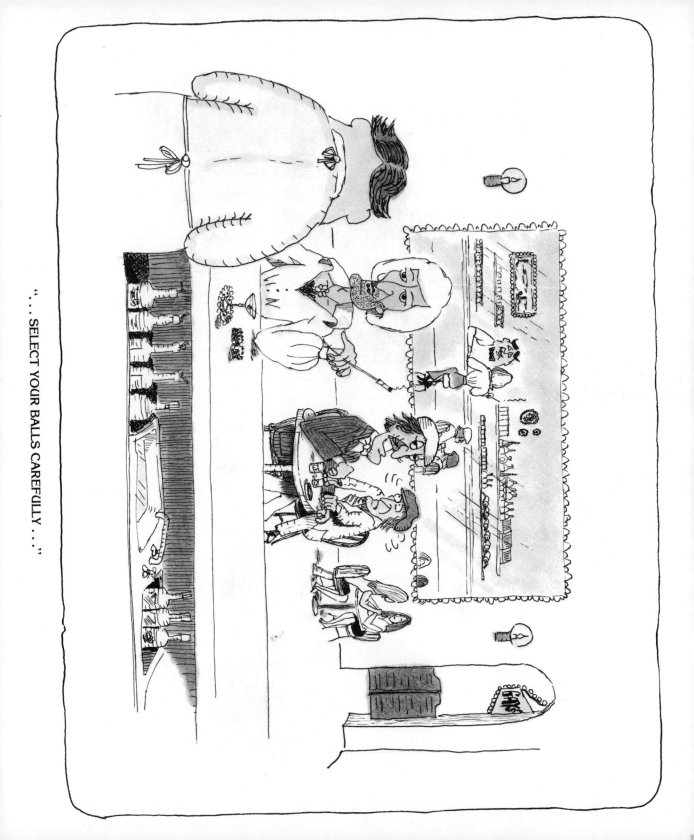

"... SELECT YOUR BALLS CAREFULLY ..."

# PART TWO

## HOW TO SWING

The development of an unfailing swing requires hours of diligent practice. Many participants seem to have lost sight of this and their desire to tee it up without sufficient preparation usually spells disaster on the front side. Often the damage is irrecoverable on the back side and double bogeys become the order of the day . . . or night, depending on your starting time.

## TAKING HOLD OF YOUR CLUB

The one thing that most determines how well you're going to score is the way in which you hold your club.

The coupling between you and your club has to be just right or you haven't a chance.

There are three basic types of grip: The overlapping grip, the interlocking grip, and the baseball grip. They will all feel awkward at first, but stick with one, keeping the "V's" formed by thumbs and forefingers pointing between your chin and right shoulder, and your hands will be in the correct position for whatever shot you might want to try.

"THERE ARE THREE BASIC TYPES OF GRIP . . ."

# YOUR STANCE

Smooth balanced footwork is the foundation of a good swing.

Keep the stance as narrow as possible for, surprisingly enough, you can actually swing harder with the feet-together stance than you can with the straddle-legged stance. However, this should not be confused with the closed stance which tends to restrict proper hip action, often resulting in a blocked shot that could take you out of play.

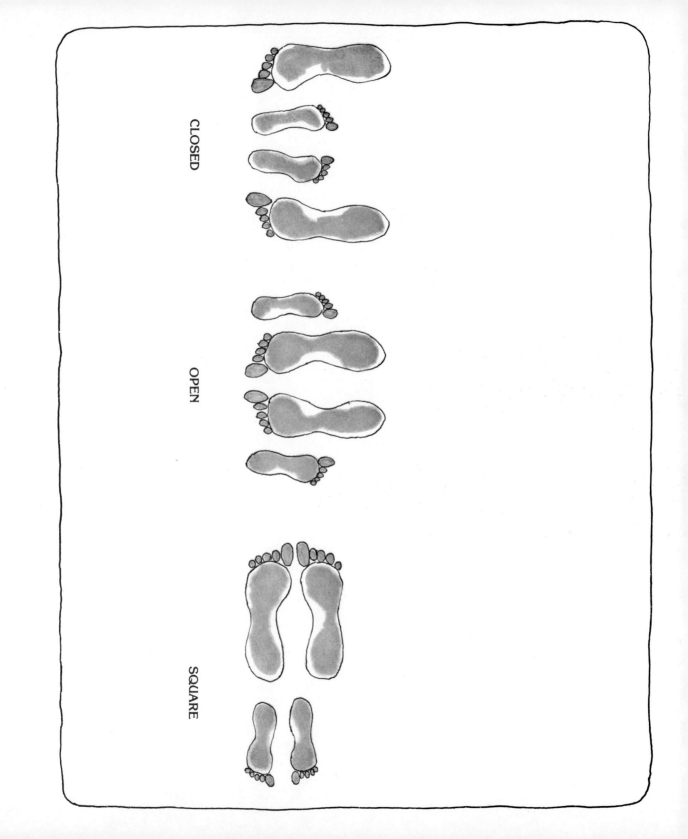

# SWINGING

The most common fault many of us fall into is over-swinging. This one bad habit has probably ruined more potentially good swingers than anything else. You must learn to swing within your own limitations and the place to discipline yourself is in your backswing.

After a preliminary waggle many players like to get things started with a forward press. A smooth forward press should put you in excellent shape to begin backswinging. But this is where you have to be careful, for taking your club past horizontal will usually cause premature uncocking starting down. This early release of energy will result in a terrific loss of power in the hitting zone.

You will undoubtedly hear of those who do swing past horizontal and even get away with it. They are able to do this by holding on and not letting go too soon. The concentration and training required to delay release until the very last possible moment is what separates the sensuous swinger from the mere passable player.

"YOU MUST LEARN TO SWING WITHIN YOUR OWN LIMITATIONS . . ."

## SLICING AND HOOKING

The most prevalent mistake almost every beginner makes is swinging from outside-to-inside. This inevitably produces a bad slice, or a large hotel bill.

However, you can lose that swing pattern by learning to be a hooker. A good way to begin is to practice swinging from inside-to-outside. This will generally give you a hook, if not a cold.

As you can see, neither slicing nor hooking are particularly helpful, except when needed to get out of some unfortunate lie, or around some obstacle blocking your approach home.

# THE PROPER APPROACH

The strokes played from around the apron are more often than not the determining factor in how well you'll score.

**THE PITCH**—A good way to get things off the ground in a hurry. There are times when only a smooth pitch, delivered with finesse, will put you in scoring range. This type of approach should put you close enough to make your next stroke practically a gimme.

**THE CHIP**—This is much lower than the pitch and is certainly the more down to earth approach. Those who frequently employ it are usually known as **chippers** . . . or **chippies,** depending on the action.

# PRODIGIOUS PUTTING

It is ironic but most big swingers are not passionate putters. In truth, you really have to be square to consistently get it down in the fewest number of strokes.

Your eyes must be squarely over the ball. Your clubface must be square to your intended line. And the more often you can strike your putts squarely on that sweet spot, the greater success you're bound to have in rolling them in, from any distance.

To find your putter's sweet spot, let it hang free, then tap the face until you find a spot where the tap doesn't turn it. That's either your sweet spot or a very sore one.

There are several things you should consider before you step up to knock it in. First, you should examine the shot from all sides. Second, study the contour, speed, grain, and texture of the turf. The time spent here will more than pay off in strokes saved later.

"... YOU SHOULD EXAMINE THE SHOT FROM ALL SIDES."

# PRACTICE MAKES PERFECT

Practice for a purpose, to correct some fault or improve some part of your game.

Start easy with some soft niblicking before attempting any mashie play.

If you're not getting the distance you think you should, try using more leg action, driving the knees forward. Dig in and push with the right foot at impact. Don't expect miracles.

Work on all the kinds of shots you might have to resort to during play. Remember, there's more than one way to play a bunker shot!

"REMEMBER, THERE'S MORE THAN ONE WAY TO PLAY A BUNKER SHOT!"

# PART THREE

## PLAYING THE GAME

Unless one is content to be but a voyeur, improving one's skills by merely watching the pros do their stuff, then there is no better way to sharpen your game and keep your rhythm than by going out to play as often as possible.

Practicing by yourself will only give you so much feel. After that your game must be honed in actual competition where every stroke counts.

But your final score shouldn't be your only consideration. After all, "It is better to have bogeyed and lost than never to have bogeyed at all."

# KINDS OF PLAY—MATCH AND MEDAL

Match play and medal play are the two ways one can play the game.

Medal play or stroke play, as it is more popularly known, determines a winner by a player's total number of strokes against the field. This is the most popular form of play in large events where a great number of spectators have to be considered.

The more personal and exciting form of play, at least for the participants themselves, is match play. This is head to head combat, one on one—or sometimes two on two—where being able to outmaneuver and shake up your opponent can win you the hole and, if enough of them, the match!

There are many different kinds of match play and we will define some of the ones most prevalent in our society today.

**SINGLES MATCH**—Simply one player against another.

**TWOSOME**—This is usually just two people who enjoy playing with each other. If things should get out of hand, there's no law that says it can't turn into a match.

**THREESOME**—Three persons playing together. Either that or two on one.

**THREE-BALL**—This is where three play against one another, each playing their own game. Can also be called a round-robin, menage d'trois . . .

**FOURSOME**—Can be as simple as four persons playing together, or as perverted as two against two, with partners alternating strokes until one holes out.

**FOUR-BALL**—This is where two play their better score, by holes, against the better score of two other players. More popularly called best-ball . . . or an orgy.

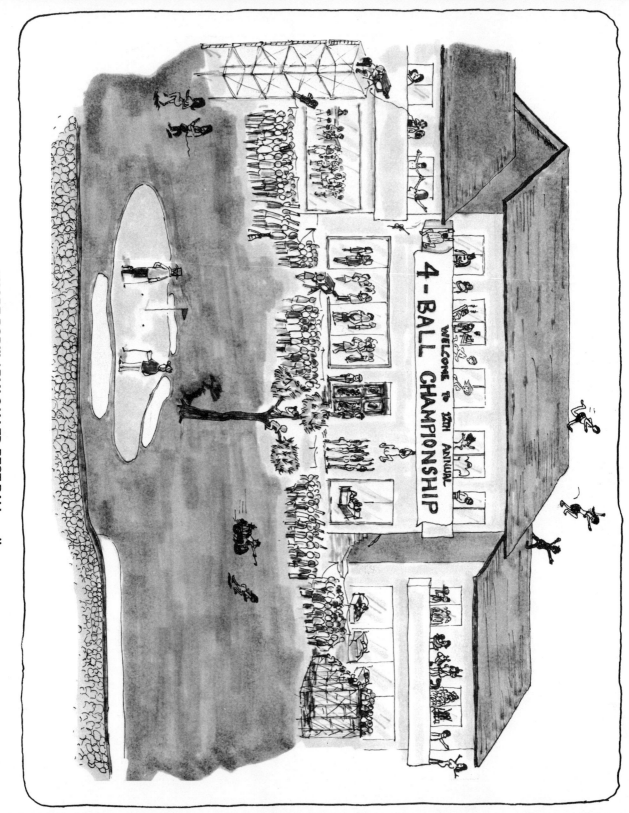

"MORE POPULARLY CALLED BEST-BALL . . . ."

# GETTING A STARTING TIME

This is not always the easiest thing to do. There are millions of swingers across the United States and for many of them the weekend is the only time they can get away from their wives and kids and play a round.

Obviously more of us would prefer to swing in private than in public. But if this type of layout is financially out of the question, then you must seek another course of action . . . perhaps one lighted for night play.

Because these layouts invariably breed slow play, you must usually make a reservation in advance if you expect to get a complete round in before daybreak.

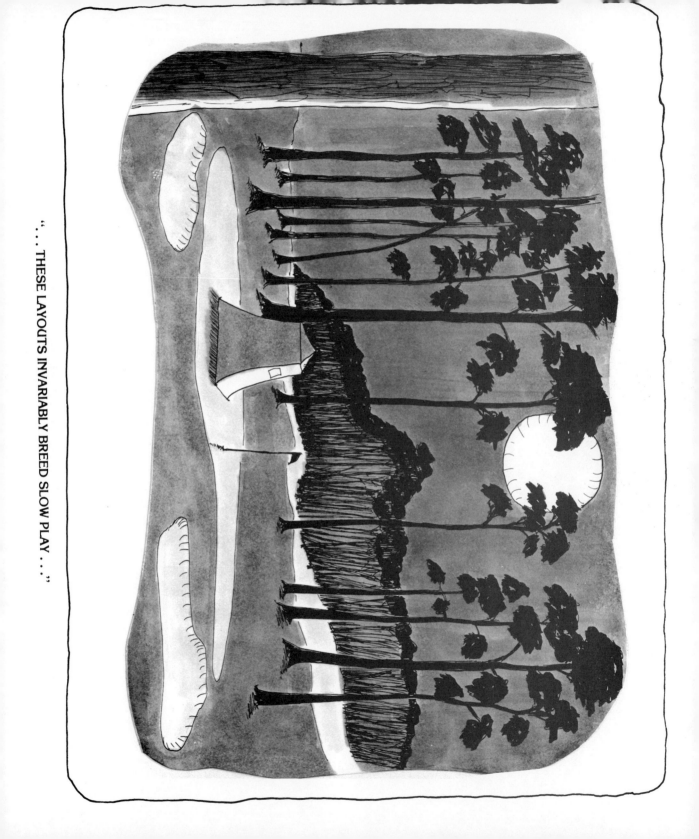

"... THESE LAYOUTS INVARIABLY BREED SLOW PLAY ..."

# GETTING IT OFF THE TEE

There's no question that one of the greatest thrills in the game is getting a long one off at the beginning of play. Some pointers that will help you accomplish this:

**TEE IT HIGH**—Catching your ball on the upstroke always provides more distance.

**DELAY UNCOCKING**—By delaying uncocking until the clubhead reaches the hitting zone, you will be assured of achieving the greatest clubhead speed at impact.

**DON'T TRY TO KILL IT**—Swing easily and let the club do the job and you'll be surprised how much more distance you'll get.

If you find yourself up against some really big knockers and you've got to let out the shaft, try to remember, "It's not how long you make it, it's how you make it long."

**TIME TO PUT IT AWAY**—When your driver sours and you just can't get it out there like you used to, give it a rest.

"WHEN YOUR DRIVER SOURS . . . ."

# PLAY IT AS IT LAYS

Once off the tee you may find your ball in any number of positions, from uphill and downhill lies to sidehill lies.

On sidehill lies always aim to the high side (trust me) and on uphill or downhill lies always position your ball closer to the higher foot, let your swing follow the slope, and let your conscience be your guide.

In the long run you are bound to score more upsets and win more tight ones if you can learn to get it up and down from any position, no matter how hazardous.

32

" . . . LEARN TO GET IT UP AND DOWN FROM ANY POSITION . . . "

## YOU GOT TROUBLE MY FRIENDS

Being able to play out of trouble without penalty will show the opposition what kind of a competitor you really are. You may even surprise yourself.

The first thing to remember is NEVER GIVE UP. You may not be in as much trouble as you think. If you are and you decide to gamble, think first of what other trouble you might be getting yourself into.

Always try to visualize the shot you want to make. Getting a clear mental picture of how the stroke should be played will give you the confidence to play it. But don't think about the outcome or strain to see where your ball goes. You'll find out, soon enough.

**DON'T FENCE ME IN**—If you should find yourself really up against it, you may have no other recourse but a backward shot between the legs.

**TALKING TO THE TREES**—When playing from the trees, consider other players' position before taking relief.

**IN A WATER HAZARD**—If any part of your ball is above the water, then you may possibly have a shot at it. If, however, your ball is submerged, you might just as well accept your fate and throw in the towel.

**STYMIED**—There are times when it becomes obvious that there's just no way to get through. You should not be ashamed at having to take a step back to get a better angle—as long as it doesn't take you completely out of play.

**OFF A BARE SURFACE**—This is a very delicate shot and must be executed with the utmost care for both the top of the backswing, as well as the bare bottom.

**OBSTRUCTIONS**—You may get relief from anything artificial whether erected, placed, or left in the area of play. No penalty . . . at least not in this life.

# THE RUB OF THE GREEN

As you approach the putting surface be aware of its contours relative to your ball and the hole. Examine the grass to see which way the grain lies. If it's shiny, the grain is with you. If it's dark, it's probably against you.

Approach your putt on a line with the hole and check for any deviation from the general slope of things. Often times it's a good idea to sight from the opposite side of the hole. Some players prefer to sight from the low side. A side view doesn't hurt either and may give you a better look at the important measurements.

And always study the surface around the hole most carefully, for it can have the greatest effect on slowing putts.

"SOME PLAYERS PREFER TO SIGHT FROM THE LOW SIDE."

# USE YOUR HEAD FOR BETTER SCORING

Generally the mistakes that hurt your score are caused by not considering all the factors before you swing.

**MAKE UP YOUR MIND**—Decide on a club and convince yourself it is the right one. Remember, as long as there is some doubt in your mind, it's almost impossible to make your usual swing—though sometimes you'd be better off with an unusual one.

**SELF CONTROL**—Many players tend to get careless when they get ahead. Others lose their rhythm when they get behind. Whatever position you find yourself in, don't let the ups and downs of the game make you lose your cool.

**CONCENTRATE**—Play your own game. It will be easier to stay loose if you concentrate on what you are doing; let your adversary do the watching and worrying.

Above all, try to play each stroke and hole as it comes, as if it were the only stroke and hole you were going to play all day.

"... DON'T LET THE UPS AND DOWNS OF THE GAME MAKE YOU LOSE YOUR COOL."

# PART FOUR

# RULES AND
# ETIQUETTE

Over the years the truly great swingers have always had the highest regard for fair play and sportsmanlike conduct.

In spite of this fine example many players still think that swearing and beating their club over a lost ball will bring it back. It won't. If you lose your ball, accept the penalty and try to keep a stiff upper lip . . . if nothing else.

# RULES AND PENALTIES

The rules of play provide you with certain rights and definite wrongs. Penalties can range anywhere from loss of the hole to adding one or two strokes to your score. The mature swinger will take such penalties in stride, learning from his mistakes. After all, the more strokes penalized, the more you get to play!

OUT OF BOUNDS

CLEANING OF BALL

A LOST BALL

PLAYING THE WRONG BALL

CASUAL WATER

PLAYING OUT OF TURN

BALL UNFIT FOR PLAY

UNPLAYABLE LIE

# WINTER RULES AND OTHER FOUL PLAY

Winter rules, or preferred lies, generally result when playing conditions become so hazardous that only by improving your lie will you be able to play at all. After spending a great deal of time and effort setting up a terrific match, most of you certainly aren't about to give up the game just because of a few storm warnings on the home front.

**SWINGING IN THE RAIN**—Be prepared and carry large towels, rubbers, and extra gloves. A handkerchief wrapped around the shaft will help when the grip is wet, or use rosin to keep hands from slipping. Remember the turf will be softer, so make sure your feet are firmly planted so you won't slip as you try to bang it hole high.

**FRIGID CONDITIONS**—You should be aware that extremely cold weather can freeze your balls to such an extent that a noticeable loss of distance will result. To compensate for this many players wrap their balls in a heating pad before what could be a chilly round. The consensus of pros and amateurs alike seems to be that indeed, warm balls do go farther.

"... WARM BALLS DO GO FARTHER."

# HANDICAPPING THE PLAYERS

Rarely do both participants in a match possess the same ability and experience necessary to execute all the strokes from all the positions. Fortunately, through the handicapping system, swingers with a wide variance in scoring ability can still compete against one another on a fairly equal basis.

To find out your handicap first take the lowest 10 of your last 20 scores. If that's a problem, then 5 of your last 10 scores . . . Two and a half of your last 5?

Then subtract the rating of the layout—assuming all scores were made on the same layout. You should try to stick with one course until you've established your handicap. Your handicap would be determined by adding all vital statistics, dividing by 3, and then multiplying by 85 per cent.

The ideal situation would be for everyone to be a card-carrying player so that before you tee off you have to show your handicap to the opposition. In this way the strokes would fall where they may and you'd probably have one helluva close and thrilling match. Who knows, you might even have to go extra holes!

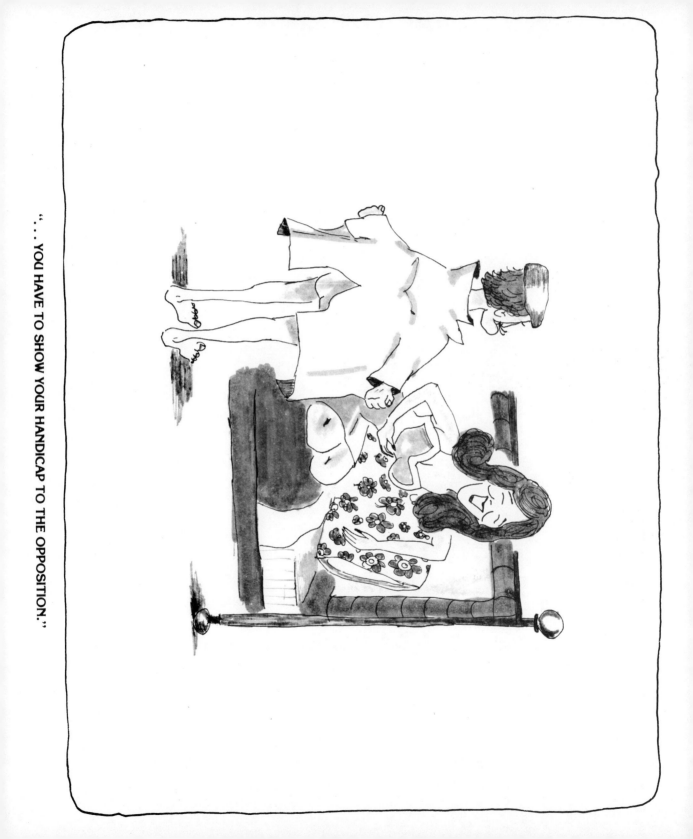

"... YOU HAVE TO SHOW YOUR HANDICAP TO THE OPPOSITION."

# SOME BASIC COURTESIES

You'll enjoy the exercise much more and not prevent others from enjoying it if you keep the following in mind.

1.  Replace divots.

2.  Repair ball marks on the putting surface.

3.  Play without undue delay. Be ready when it's your turn and don't waste time with a lot of ball washing and small talk.

If there's an open hole ahead, invite those waiting to play through.

Leave the area immediately after holing out. Mark your score later.

With so many variables such as speedy youngsters, slow seniors, calm or stormy playing conditions, the cost of the layout . . . it's difficult to establish a time limit on play. However, most players would agree that a single round that takes five hours or longer can be a real pain in the ass.

"LEAVE THE AREA IMMEDIATELY AFTER HOLING OUT. MARK YOUR SCORE LATER."

# PART FIVE

# THE 19th HOLE

Obviously, we have not tackled every aspect of the sport. The last three chapters will only partially rectify that. After all, some things are better left to the individual players' ingenuity and imagination.

# KEEPING SCORE

The next time somebody asks for your score, and you're ready to burst out with all the excuses: the bad lies, the traps you got into, old equipment . . . you would do well to remember the immortal words of Brigham Young who said: "It's not how, it's how many!"

But scoring a hole-in-one is by no means the whole ball game. To the real sport half the fun is getting there . . . sometimes more!

"IT'S NOT HOW, IT'S HOW MANY!"

# THE SENIOR SWINGER

In your senior years it often becomes difficult to hold onto your timing. Your stamina isn't what it used to be and though your heart may be in it, the game seems a whole lot tougher than before.

It is NOT the end of the line! With a few adjustments and the desire to still take a whack at it, you may even IMPROVE on your scoring ability.

First, your equipment. To give you the added distance you've probably lost over the years, try longer and whippier shafts.

Perfect your short game because it's played in the scoring area where physical strength does not count as much. This can save your back muscles over the long haul.

Relax by taking deep breaths and waggling your club and wiggling your feet just before you swing.

Don't be surprised if your years of experience should really pay off. The smooth and confident stroke, not to mention the smile and savoir-faire of an older player is a combination that the younger competition may find hard to beat when it comes to getting close on these newer stretched out jobs.

After all it takes years of blood, sweat, and tears to win the affection of a large and loyal "gal'ry."

"PERFECT YOUR SHORT GAME . . ."

# TIME TO SEE A PRO?

When your game sours, you should not hesitate to see a pro. You may find one who gives group lessons. But if these should make you self-conscious and you can afford private lessons, then by all means, that's the way to go.

A good pro will give playing lessons. Pro-am matches are more popular than ever, though getting into one with a famous touring pro can be expensive. But the experience is usually well worth the price. Generally the pro will take the time to tell you how and what to work on in your play. If they get familiar enough, they may even suggest a different type of ball.

However, in the long run, it's your local pro that will straighten you out more often than not. Some of them will even set up a game for you if you have no one to play with.

And if your neighborhood pros are really on the ball, they may even want to video tape you in action. But a word of caution here, for often the pro that is anxious to see you swing on instant replay may be just as eager to replay your scoring achievements to the local papers. And then you may come to feel "the rub of the green" as you've never felt it before.

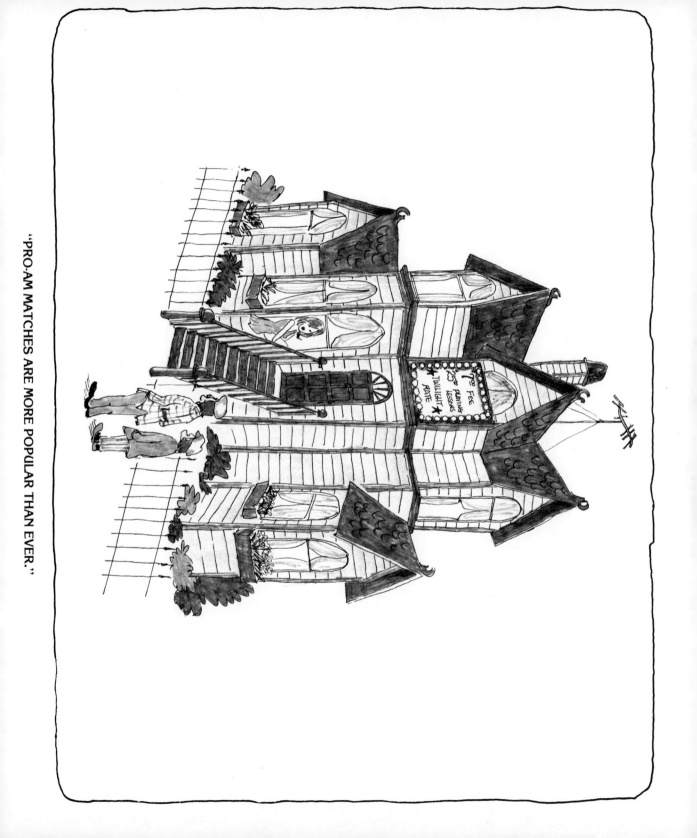

"PRO-AM MATCHES ARE MORE POPULAR THAN EVER."

# GOLF GRAFFITI*

*or Everything You Always Wanted To Know About Foreplay.

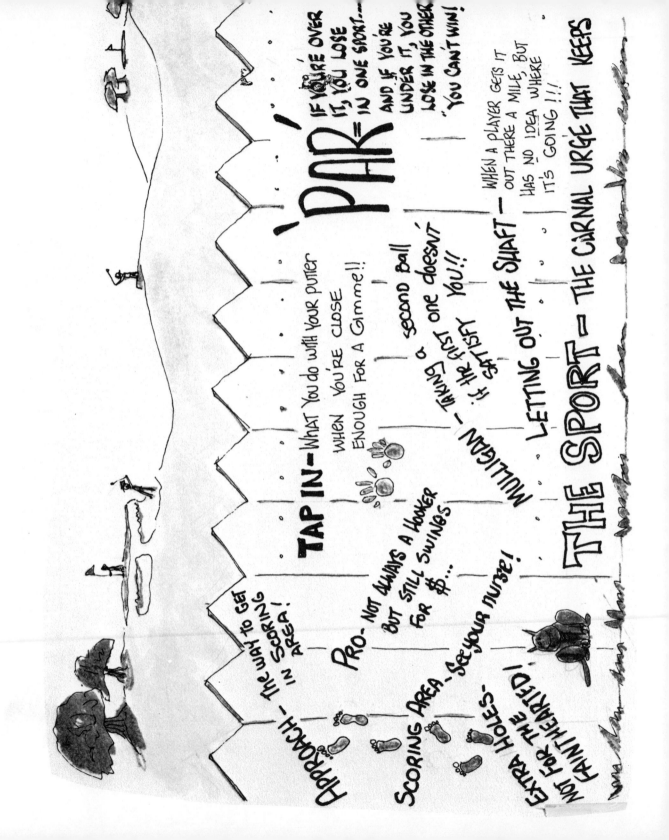

**'PAR** = IF YOU'RE OVER IT, YOU LOSE IN ONE SPORT... AND IF YOU'RE UNDER IT, YOU LOSE IN THE OTHER! 'YOU CAN'T WIN!

**TAP IN** - WHAT YOU DO WITH YOUR PUTER WHEN YOU'RE CLOSE ENOUGH FOR A GIMME!!

**PRO** - NOT ALWAYS A HOOKER, BUT STILL SWINGS FOR $...

**MULLIGAN** - TAKING A SECOND BALL IF THE FIRST ONE DOESN'T SATISFY YOU!!

**LETTING OUT THE SHAFT** - WHEN A PLAYER GETS IT OUT THERE A MILE, BUT HAS NO IDEA WHERE IT'S GOING !!!

**THE SPORT** = THE CARNAL URGE THAT KEEPS

**APPROACH** - THE WAY TO GET IN SCORING AREA!

**SCORING AREA** - SEE YOUR NURSE!

**EXTRA HOLES** - NOT FOR THE FAINTHEARTED!

# OTHER GOLF BOOKS BY MARK OMAN

## The 9 Commandments of Golf... According to The Pro Upstairs—Cosmic Secrets for Mastering the Game!

Illustrated by Doug Goodwin
(112 pages—20 illustrations) ISBN 0-917236-07-6    $6.95

Discover the glory of golf, as it is in Heaven and ought to be on Earth!

*"A lot of God's ideas for Earth haven't always worked out. Take that Moses thing... You haven't even gotten the 10 Commandments right yet! God knows what you'll do with 9 Commandments just for golf... Actually, even He doesn't know. But He's got to try something!!"*

**The Pro Upstairs**

## How To Live With A Golfaholic—A Survival Guide for Family And Friends of Passionate Players

Illustrated by Jay Campbell and Carl Christ
(96 pages—20 illustrations) ISBN 0-917346-14-9    $6.95

The only book to help you survive the traps and hazards of a golfer's magnificent obsession.

*"Mark Oman's observations are all in the birdie circle."*

**Charles M. Schulz**

## Portrait Of A Golfaholic

Illustrated by Gary Patterson
(96 pages—30 illustrations) ISBN 0-8092-5335-6    $6.95

The bible of Golfaholics Anonymous. A look into the wide world of golfaholism.

*"A great gift to the guy in your foursome who is always pressing for 6 A.M. tee times...Every sinner loves company."*

**Los Angeles Times**

★ ★ ★ ★